T0197485

O.L. HARRISON

A Christmas from Heaven

To order additional copies of this book, contact:
Xlibris
844-714-8691
www.Xlibris.com
Orders@Xlibris.com

ISBN: Softcover   978-1-6698-1494-8
        EBook   978-1-6698-1495-5

Print information available on the last page

Rev. date: 03/10/2022

It was the night before Christmas and all through the house was as quiet as a mouse. Suddenly I was awakened by a small still voice that called my name.

"Johnny, Johnny, wake up," the voice spoke to me. "Get up, for I have many gifts under my tree for thee."

I quickly rushed out of my bed, put my slippers and robe on, and dashed down the stairs. What I saw was so amazing and bright. Gifts filled the room--what a sight! I held my mouth with such a surprise, so many gifts filled the room underneath of the tree. My mom had named the tree earlier the Blood of Jesus Tree. I then ran over to find my name. *Every gift I touched had my name on it.*

I began to open one gift at a time; the first gift was so divine. Out poured inspirational words spoken in the atmosphere that God is here. With great anticipation, I opened one more, and this gift had songs of joy with doves flying out. The third gift was everlasting life; I fell to my knees with such great joy! The gifts I opened up next had strength, hope, kindness, peace, good health, prosperity, every needs met, wisdom with understanding, grace, love, mercy, and every healing gift of every disease. My heart so rejoiced that I serve such an awesome God.

My parents and my brothers were awakened by the sound of music that filled the air.

"Wow!" They were surprised!

As each of them touched a gift, their names appeared. When our little brother, Emmanuel, touched a gift, a toy sometimes popped out. We all received clothes, shoes, and items that each of us needed. Each time we picked up a gift, another would appear.

When my mom went into the kitchen, a spread of all kinds of food was there. My father received a key, therefore he didn't open any more.

My father went to get my aunt out of the room (as she had been sick). She picked up a gift, and she received healing and good health. We all shouted with joy. Truly, this was a Christmas from heaven.

We all joined hands and began to worship God. At the end of the worship, my father prayed and said, "We *must share* our blessings with our neighbors as we still had so many gifts under the tree, after we eat this delicious food that God had prepared for us." We sat down to eat and said our grace; the *food was the best ever.*

We all got dressed and headed outdoors, stacking our new red wagons with gifts from under the tree.

Wow! A *new van* was sitting in front of our house. My father said God had provided as our old van was on it's very last leg.

Knocking on neighbors' doors, we shared the gifts we had received, and the word spread from neighbor to neighbor.

The people came to our house. Everyone wanted to see the Blood of Jesus Tree and receive their gifts. There was so much love shared that the good news reached other communities and countries all over the world. Truly, this was a Christmas from heaven!

My great-great-great-grandfather told this story to his children, and now, four generations later, I am sharing it with you!

Hope you enjoyed! I am Johnny IV.

Printed in the United States
by Baker & Taylor Publisher Services